The dinosaurs are having a party

It isn't too far on the bus

The house is vibrating and shaking

But the neighbours aren't making a fuss.

A **big** dinosaur appears by the door

He smiles and says "Hello.

There are **plenty** of meat eaters in here

Are you **SURE** you want to go?"

Dear Special Guest

You are invited to the dinos-
dinner at the dinos-
aurs' party at 3pm
on Saturday.

Yours Mr T. Rex
xx

The dinosaurs are having a party

Some are extremely tall

Others inside are terribly **wide**

So I SQUEEZE my way through the hall.

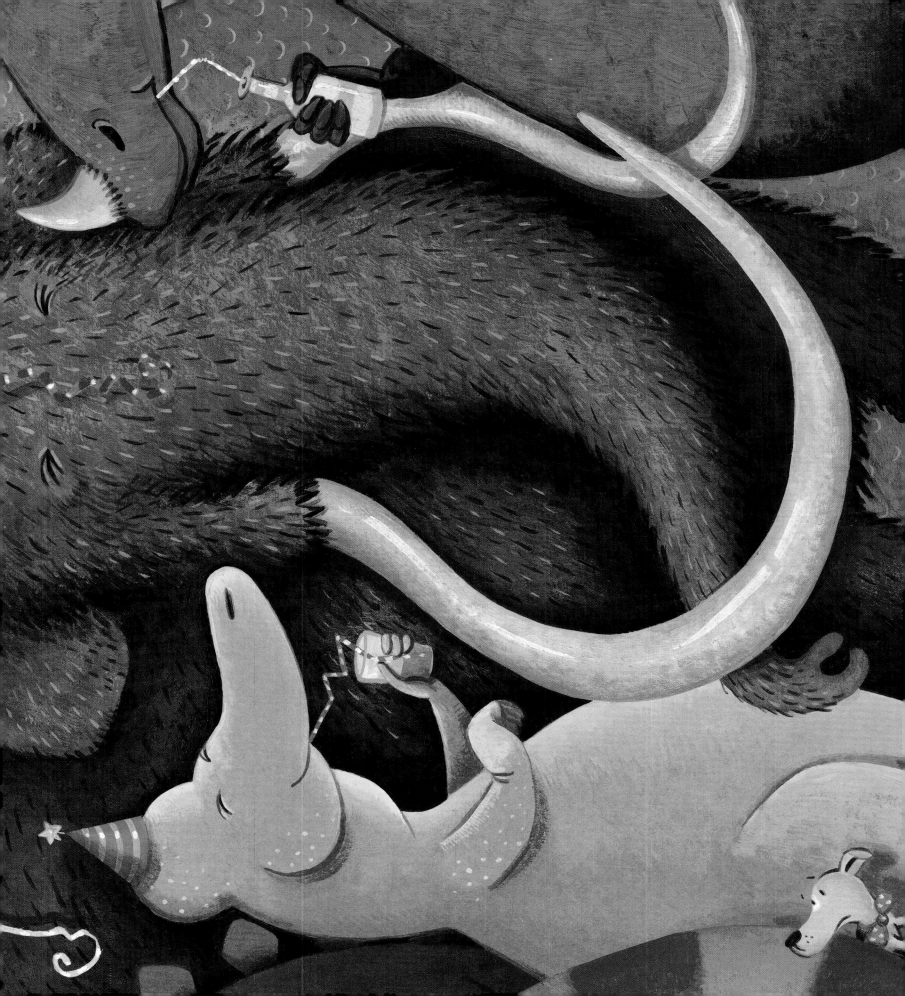

Stepping inside one of the rooms

There's a game of musical chairs

A little one loses and wails,

"Not fair! Nobody cares!"

So they change instead to musical **bumps**

The music suddenly stops

The little one looks like he's winning . . . .

Till he's squished by a triceratops.

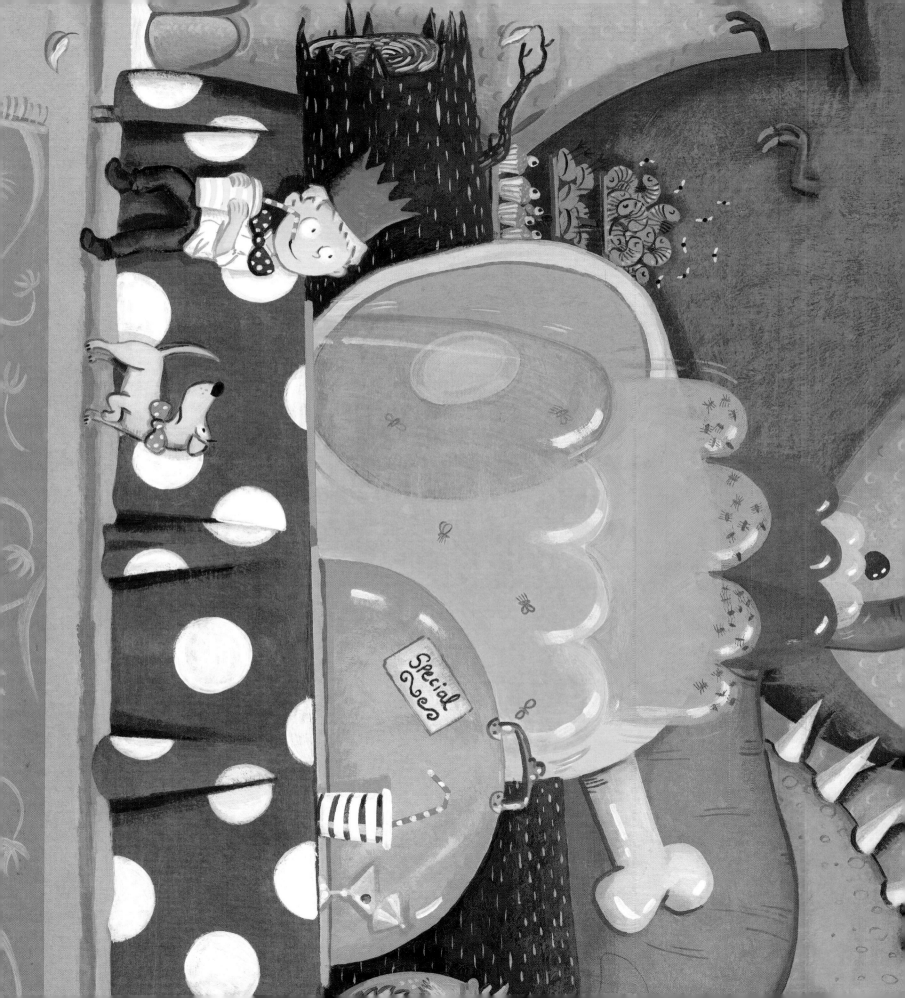

The dinosaurs are having a party

There's plenty of food to gobble

There are jellies of every flavour

Though **something** is making them **wobble.**

There's a barbecue in the back garden

Though I can't see a morsel of meat

The cook suggests I sit down

But I don't like the look of the seat.

The bouncy castle is lots of fun

For the whole of the dinosaur gang

Until a **huge** stegosaurus **jumps** on

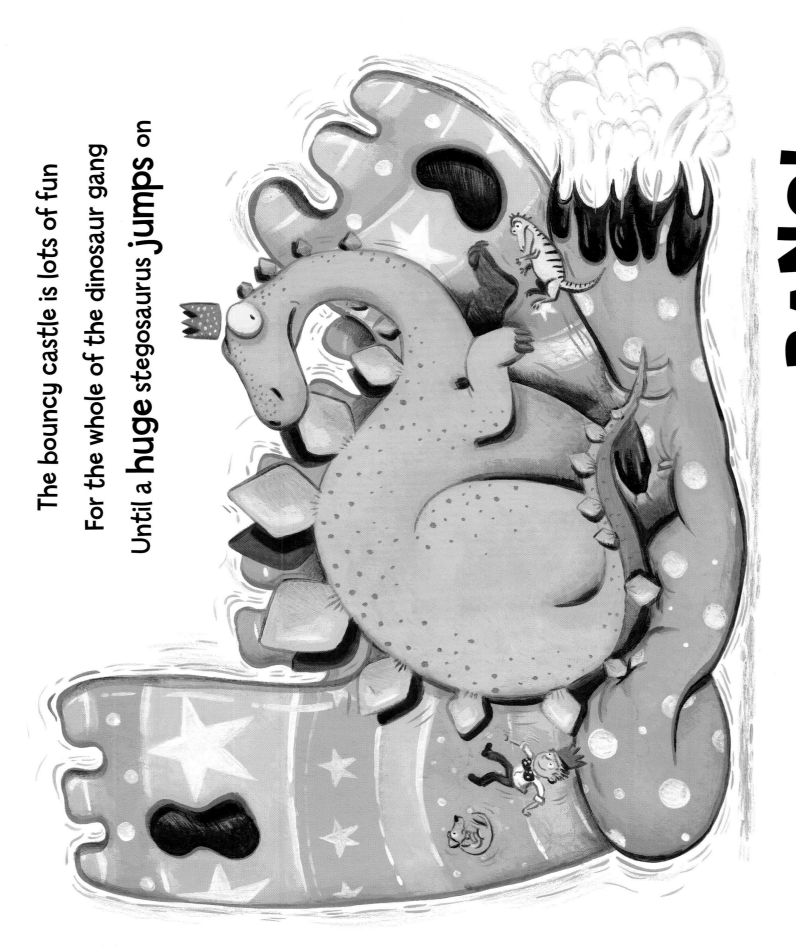

And **bursts** the whole thing with a **BANG!**

There's a really long queue for the toilet

Someone is being too slow

One desperate dinosaur's shouting,

"Hurry up. We all need to go!"

Someone is flushing the toilet

Then slowly pushing the door

A terrible pong **spills** out

Then . . . . . .

Occupie

Roasting today
* Special Guest *
BBQ dinner from our
Chef Alfonsaurus
a delicious
delicacy
something to get your teeth into

T-Rex steps out with a

Poodri!

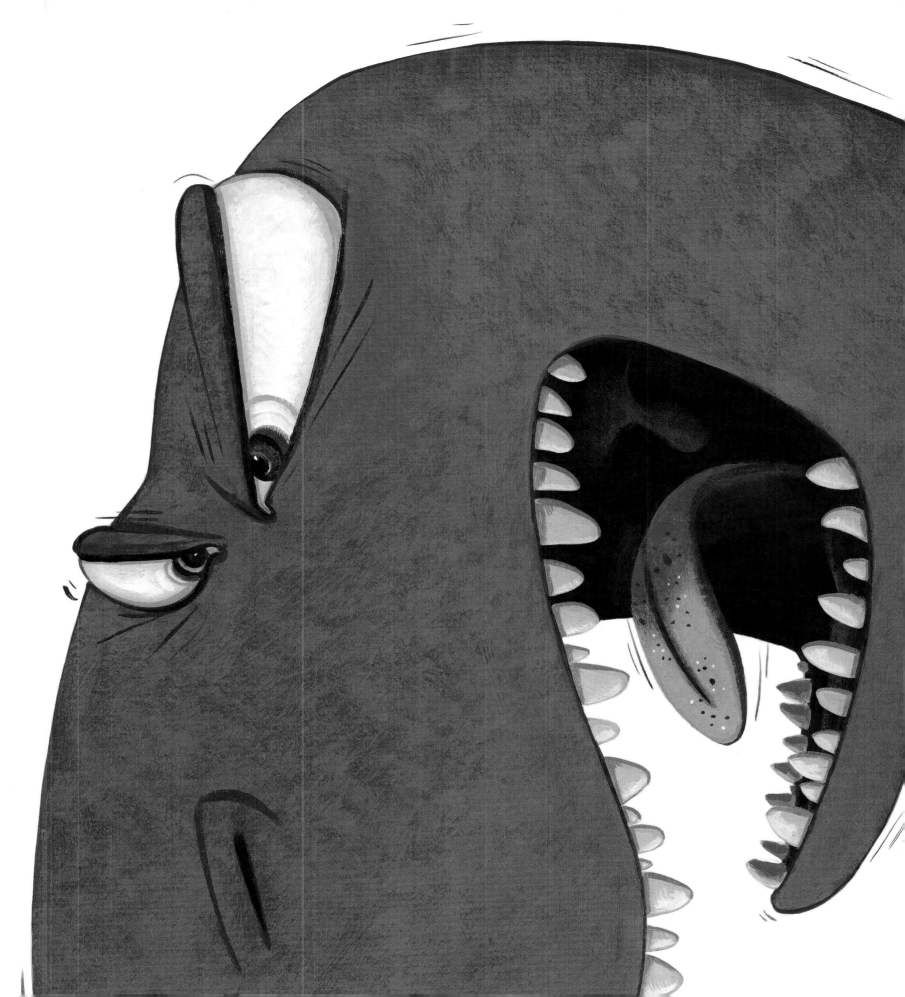

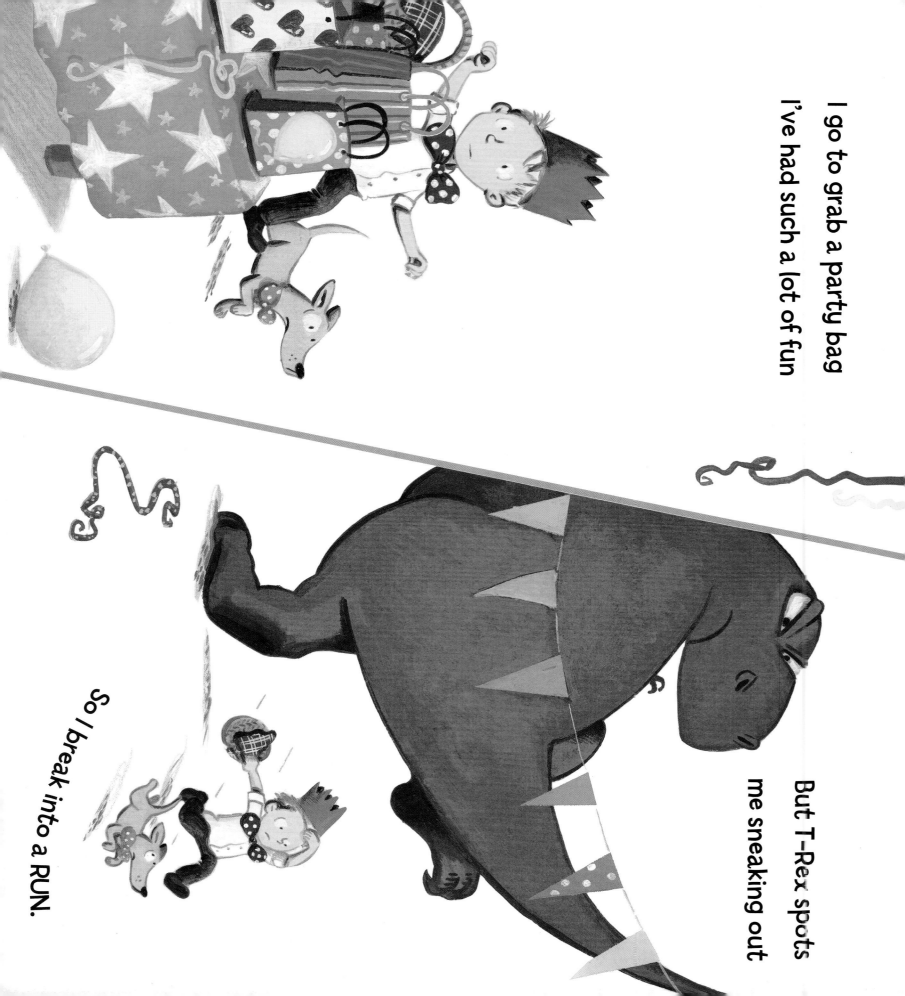

I go to grab a party bag
I've had such a lot of fun

But T-Rex spots
me sneaking out

So I break into a RUN.

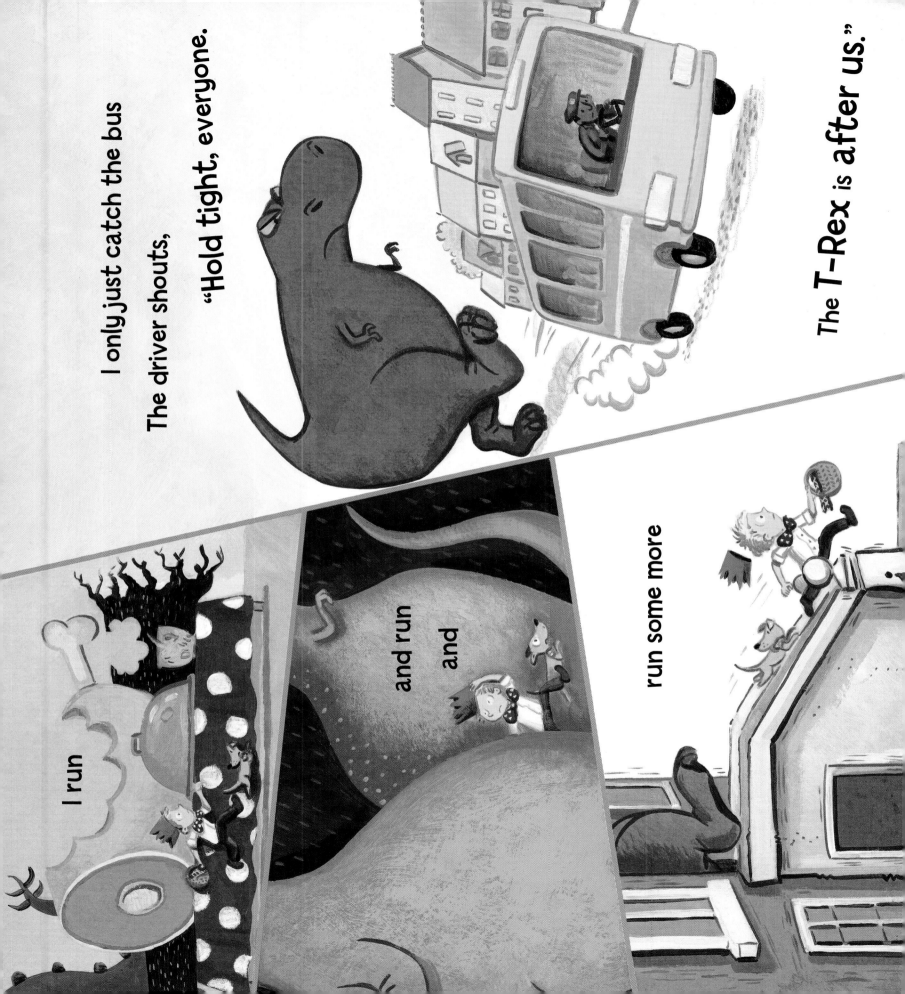

I only just catch the bus

The driver shouts,

"Hold tight, everyone."

The T-Rex is after us."

I run

and run

and

run some more

The driver turns left,

then right,

then left

Trying his best
to confuse him.

Hurrah! we finally lose him!

He goes round
and round
in circles . . .

I mostly enjoyed the dinosaurs' party
There is just one little snag.
I don't think the bag I picked up . . .

Was really a **PARTY BAG!**